# KISS THE DUKE GOODBYE

TRACY SUMNER

Kiss the Duke Goodbye

Copyright © 2024 by Tracy Sumner

Editor: Victory Editing

Cover designer: Swoonies Romance Art

All rights reserved.

No part of this book may be reproduced in any form or by any electronic or mechanical means, including information storage and retrieval systems, without written permission from the author, except for the use of brief quotations in a book review.

*Love betters what is best.*
*~William Wordsworth*

The Troublesome Trio
Knox

tightly as barnacles to a ship's hull. Taking him down with them.

His gaze fell to the Drury Lane placard in the shop window. He smiled softly as he noted the artist's initials sketched in the corner, recalling why he'd come to be in such dire financial straits aside from his horror of a father landing him there. His youngest brother, Damien, had needed ready cash to enable him to secure the woman of his heart. Of his *choosing*.

If Knox did nothing else in this life, he would ensure his family's happiness—after he'd done too little in his youth to safeguard it. He believed in true love, therefore relieving the Earl of Whitmore of his debts so Damien would be free to marry his daughter, Mercy, hadn't caused Knox one moment's hesitation. A duke's support also allowed Mercy the freedom to pursue art without fear of society's recrimination.

However, his solicitors weren't so idealistic.

A stinging gust whipped down the street and into the open neck of his greatcoat. As he curled his fingers around his lapels, either he shifted or the moon did, and there she was, standing in a rippling wash of light on the other side of the window.

Clarissa Marlowe, his secret, brilliant fascination.

Unlike his reckless twin, Cortland, Knox didn't move, gesture, or call out to her. He let his attraction muscle through him like a shot of whisky. Some called him a brooder, an overthinker, but he rather believed he had the edge, savoring life in contemplative moments exactly like these. Relishing the rush that hit him. The certainty.

Clarissa's serviceable gown encased her slender figure like liquid stardust, better than any from the finest modiste in London. And her eyes, *oh*, they were always a surprise. A jolt, a pleasure. Sometimes the pale gray of a winter morning, others the shimmering pewter of a stormy sky. He wondered what he'd have to do to make them change at his command. A thought that made him hot beneath the collar and the waistband.

Too, her smile, which she rarely offered, tightened his chest like a metal clasp had been clinched around it. No female in London, not *one*, made him feel like a boy skipping down the Hampstead lanes of his youth. That time, last spring, when he'd shared the story of Viscount Henry tumbling from his horse in Hyde Park, Miss Marlowe had laughed, a *real* laugh. A dimple, tiny and perched at the outer edge of her lips, flared to life, nearly sending him to his knees.

It was then he realized he was in danger of falling for a woman unsuited to his future.

In standing and, sadly, in wealth.

He was embarrassed to be such a cliché, the impoverished duke in need of a plump dowry. Thankfully, he supposed, he wasn't going to have any difficulty finding an heiress or an earl's daughter, a widowed countess or a baroness. While the woman he coveted, the one standing on the other side of the glass, seemed uninterested in him. Clearly indifferent, in fact. Like a fool, he kept coming to her shop without a hint of encouragement. His brothers had finally told him their wives didn't need another bonnet, not in this lifetime.

So, he'd begun handing them out to his staff.

The tumblers to the lock turned, pulling him from his musing. When Clarissa glanced around the doorframe, her face hidden in shadow, the rapid skip of Knox's heart told him he was in trouble. However, he didn't consider declining the offer to come inside, should she be prepared, after hours, to make it. He could claim the frigid weather had gotten to him.

This would be the first time she'd acknowledged any interest in him outside a paying customer. He wasn't about to let such an opportunity pass.

She beckoned, and Knox followed, stepping into a calming space redolent of dried flowers and the subtle hint of Darjeeling tea. And *her*, riding the air beneath with the call of lilies.

"Your Grace," she murmured and shut the door behind him. "I wonder at your urgent need for a bonnet at this hour. You were here five days ago if memory serves."

Chastised but remorseless, he strolled about her shop, popping his hat against his thigh. While she crossed to a covert sideboard and poured what looked to be excellent brandy into two tumblers. When she returned to him, he pondered the challenge in her gaze, the dare in the self-possessed stance of her body. He often felt like he was in competition when he visited her, like a rope was held between them, and they were each giving it a hard tug.

She tilted her head and offered the glass, lamplight shimmering off strands the color of ivory that she'd gathered into the neatest chignon in England. He'd seldom seen a more composed show of elegance in any ballroom or grand parlor.

Taking the drink, he moved to a cupboard filled with bonnets, because he'd begun to feel a primal urge to back her into a wall and either make the most heroic gamble of his life or the biggest mistake. He'd been without a woman for three months, the longest dry spell of his experience. Although it was self-imposed—and that, too, was intriguing. And frightening.

"I'm in need of a gift," he finally offered, making a

loose circle about his head with his hat. Then he sighed, realizing how silly he looked, and placed the beaver felt on a chair. "Upcoming birthday celebration I'd forgotten about. A luncheon tomorrow."

Miss Marlowe eyed him over the rim of her tumbler. "Which sister-in-law is it this time?"

He grazed his fingertip along a stunning straw creation decked out in yellow velvet. Aside from his fascination, her hats *were* the best he'd ever seen. "Baroness Crawford-Digby."

Miss Marlowe rested back against her front counter, sipping leisurely. "Ah," she said, skepticism rippling through the word.

Turning to her, he leaned his shoulder against the cupboard, hoping his irritation didn't show. His father's stern voice telling him to *remember his station* pealed through his mind. "It isn't like that. I've known the baroness's ancient goat of a husband since I was in leading strings. She's seventy if she's a day."

"I thought perhaps…" With a petite gust of laughter, she nodded to the folded broadsheet on the counter. Just yesterday, there'd been a mention of him in the *Herald's* gossip column. Some bit about an actress and the bachelor duke that was utterly baseless.

"I wish to point out, Miss Marlowe"—pausing, he tossed back the rest of her fine brandy and wiped his lips with the back of his wrist—"for the first time, I'm certain, that your judgment is incorrect."

She tipped her head in apology when she didn't seem apologetic in the least. The amusement curving her enticing lips was at his expense in every way.

"I mean…," he started, then fell silent. What was there to say? She couldn't be faulted for suspecting his motives. Undoubtedly, he had his pick of women and society found nothing more interesting than de-

was arrogant, yet adorably vulnerable. Intelligent, but not overwhelmingly so. Surly, but incredibly *kind*. She'd seen him giving shillings to the scamps in the alley on more than one occasion. Months ago, in the winter, he'd even given his coat to a beggar with a racking cough that spelled certain doom.

After one particularly vexing visit where he'd regaled her with stories from his week in the House of Lords, she'd drawn up a list of reasons why Knoxville DeWitt, the Duke of Herschel, was an impossibility. The titled gambit being number one. Two, he and his brothers, the so-called Troublesome Trio, were walking scandals. When she'd done everything possible to distance herself from a remarkable past that would be of interest to the masses should they find out about it. Of interest to the man standing before her with a gaining-fury scowl on his face.

His eyes glowed, an opaque, emerald wonder as they took her in. "You've been propositioned?" He tapped his ear with the heel of his hand, the garnet stone in his signet ring glimmering. "Did I hear that right?"

She reclaimed her glass to keep her hands off him. His chest beneath superfine had been as hard as the marble sculptures in the British Museum, his hip where it bumped hers a point of enticing exchange. If she fantasized about lying beneath his long body in her sturdy tester bed, she merely joined the ranks of many. There wasn't anything unusual about being attracted to a beautiful specimen. A man out of reach on so many levels.

Too numerous to contemplate.

Nonetheless, it was what one *did* with yearning that separated the winners from the losers. She'd learned this lesson from her mother early on.

Clarissa swallowed past her chagrin at sharing

something this private, even if the sharing was a means to an end. The end to the Duke of Herschel stopping by the Petal and Plume so often that it felt like they were becoming friends. "I've been approached, I prefer to term it. Very courteously. A brief affair without the threat of marriage. I wasn't insulted, I should say. I was flattered. It follows what I want for myself. Freedom, choice, independence."

He frowned. Coughed into his fist. Let his molten gaze touch every corner of the room before returning it to her. "Who the hell propositions someone courteously? It should involve a kiss that makes one question their next *breath*. Then no words, not one."

Blood skipping through her veins, Clarissa fidgeted, shuffling her slippers beneath her skirt. A silly habit. An *old* habit. "A nice man. An ordinary man. Not one with a page in *Debrett's*."

He laughed, a sound she'd come to know fairly well. Although this utterance had an edge. "So you want ordinary, do you?" Before she could answer, he held up his hand, halting her. His gloves were a dark gray kidskin, the color of mist off the moors. She wished for them to sweep her skin, grip her in tantalizing places, and pull her to him. "I wasn't propositioning you, by the by. I was merely inquiring about your hesitation after I asked inappropriate questions. I let emotion get the better of me. A DeWitt inclination I detest, even as I'm in the midst of doing it."

She sipped, gazing at him through the faceted crystal. The glasses had once graced the manor of an infamous viscount. She wondered what he'd say if she told him how she'd come to own them. "I shall be honest. I'm considering the offer."

The duke rocked back on his heels, his jaw muscle ticking.

"You don't agree, Your Grace?"

He blew a breath through his teeth. "Wouldn't I be the biggest hypocrite in England if I said anything against it? Not everything they write about me in the scandal sheets is false."

His admission made her furious, without reason. She'd read about the actresses, the widows, the stunning comtesse whose family had fled France. The DeWitts had stopped in her shop with their greatcoats reeking of perfume, smudges of rouge on their collars, grins of delight on their faces. This, of course, before Cort and Damien had fallen for their wives. Now, Knox was the only remaining member of the club. A lonely club, she suspected.

He took a step forward, and paused, scrubbing his hand over the back of his neck.

*Damn him,* Clarissa thought, charmed to her toes. He was nervous.

"What if I made the same offer, Miss Marlowe? Courteously and with every pledge of respect and discretion. What if I promised to make you cry out in pleasure the likes of which you've never, I pray, experienced before? And if you have, I'll vow to surpass it." He blinked, his breath hissing past his lips, his cheeks taking on a rosy tinge. "I promise to leave your legs unsteady, your heartbeat wild, your skin afire. Reason in a realm beyond. If you say yes, I will give you all I have for every second we're together. I'll let you go when you wish to leave. You'd retain your freedom, your independence, your good name. I don't want to own someone or have them own me. Nor do I want to wreck anyone, including myself."

She set her glass on the counter. This wasn't anything like Clarence Henry's politely worded suggestion that they meet at his Belgravia townhouse if she was amenable. A widower uninterested in securing

founded expression that the experiment had gone in a direction he'd not planned.

She was wholly gratified to see he'd lost control.

The man had control of far too many situations.

"Quit smiling," he ground out between lips she'd plumped with her own. "Unless you'd like me to move you atop this workspace and have you right bloody here."

Laughing, she sucked in a much-needed breath that allowed his scent into her nose, while holding on to the counter he'd threatened to place her atop to keep herself from sliding to the floor. She wondered if his sheets smelled of sandalwood and hoped she would soon find out. "Thank you, Your Grace. This was a very enlightening interview. I will consider your candidacy."

She pressed her palm to his chest, recording his heartbeat tapping beneath the heel of her hand before giving him a little shove.

He stumbled but righted himself instantly, his scowl growing. "You're not kissing the other one." He gestured between them with the glove he'd somehow hung on to during their ride. "This was enough of a test. A goddamned fire when we only needed a trifling blaze to prove anything."

She clicked her tongue against her teeth. "I think that's hardly cricket. Clarence asked first, and since I've never kissed him, I hardly know how to judge without it."

He set his jaw. "Clarence?"

"He's very nice. A cobbler."

The duke drew a fast breath through his nose. "Cobbler."

She shook out her skirt, looking down to conceal her amusement. "Good with his hands."

"Brilliant," he grumbled in a hot tone and wiggled

his glove on one delicious finger at a time. Then he was off, across the room, where he snatched up his posh hat and jammed it on his head. It sat at a horridly crooked angle Clarissa had no intention of correcting. "I suppose I'll wait with bated breath to hear your verdict."

Leaning against the counter, she took in the full picture of the Duke of Herschel in high dudgeon. *Heavens*, he was stunning, no matter how much she wished he weren't. Not to mention the bulge beneath his trouser closure her gaze kept straying to. His body was a marvel. "You're merely vexed because no one, I suspect, has ever told His Grace no."

He speared her with a leaden look that sent a quiver right through her. She was obviously attracted to the sulky ones. "You're right, they haven't. Unless you mean my father, a dreadful man who enjoyed telling me no in all kinds of hateful ways."

*Oh*, she thought. If he continued exposing fragments of himself, she feared tumbling down a slope she had no wish to traverse.

He made it to the door before his gaze sought out hers again. "And it's Knox DeWitt, Clarissa Marlowe. No more Your Grace, not one more utterance of that damned honorific. After such a blinding kiss, I think we're owed."

Then he was gone, leaving her to wilt against a workspace she'd never look at again without imagining him tupping her atop it.

## CHAPTER 2

### WHERE A VEXED MAN ACTS OUT

"The duke's in a stew," Cort murmured from his sprawl across his brother's brocade settee. He and his wife, Alex, had a newborn, and sleep was hard to find at home. "Careful what topic you bring up. I've had nothing but unkindness from his direction all morning. If it weren't as cold as a witch's teat out there and about to storm, I'd return to my loving home this very minute."

From the doorway, Damien, the youngest and most circumspect of the Troublesome Trio, narrowed his eyes as he gazed about the room, reading the situation in one astute glance. The genius in their family missed little. "Not a surprise, as I read the latest in the society column this morning. The sight of Herschel in formal blacks at the earl's ball sent Lady Dowling into a dizzy spin." Damien dusted snowflakes from his lapels and strolled into the space. "You had no choice but to grab her before she hit the marble floor."

"Nice figure, that one," Cort said from beneath the arm he'd draped across his face. "Could be worse problems than finding that sweet miss in your arms."

"Her beauty only surpassed by her immense dowry," Knox murmured, a bit queasy to realize that Lady Dowling and her bogus fainting spells might be just what his duchy's empty coffers needed. Yet, he couldn't imagine spending the rest of his life catching her as she tumbled.

"*No.*" Damien yanked off his greatcoat and hung it on the peg, the word coming out in a hardened tone he rarely used with his family. An Oxford professor, he'd returned to London yesterday for winter break. "That isn't going to happen, Knox. You marry for love or you don't marry. Spend the rest of your life with mistresses you actually like instead. Our parents' unbearable union isn't an example we're carrying into the next generation. Cort and I wed for *love*, true and lasting, as you will." He nudged his spectacles high, ever the earnest idealist. "Our steam engine investments are paying off. It's only a matter of time before we're flush with funds. A year, maybe two at the most, and we'll be golden. I've run the numbers a thousand times."

Knox tossed his quill to the massive desk that had once been his father's, sending ink across the scrambled rows of calculations gracing his ledger. "Dreamers, the lot of you. I don't have those freedoms. The staff in Hampstead, for instance, wish to be paid this year. The manor in Yorkshire requires a new roof or it will become nothing more than a handsome, medieval barn. Let's not discuss the roads in the village in Kent. The Duke of Herschel has maintained them for going on three hundred years, and I'm loathe to break the tradition."

Cort sat up, his concerned gaze meeting Knox's. Twins separated by a scant three minutes, Cort's life had been liberated by his coming in second. A veteran of Waterloo, he had scars from war but not from inherited obligation or the verbal—and occasionally physical—lashings of a man intent on preparing his son to be a duke. Knox wasn't quite sure which was worse, war or an abusive father. "We'll find a way, Knox. I've spoken to my solicitor about the investments. Money will be coming in soon."

Knox sighed and opened the top drawer of the desk. The scent of his father's tobacco drifted free, another jolt to his belly. He needed to get rid of this damned piece of jetsam. Perhaps a raging fire on the back lawn in the middle of winter wouldn't attract too much notice from the neighbors. "I've complied up a list of possibilities. Maybe it's time we discussed them."

Damien squinted, giving his spectacles a wiggle. "Possibilities?"

Cort swore and climbed to his feet. "Potential countesses, you coxcomb," he whispered and snatched the sheet of foolscap from his twin's knotted grasp.

While Cort paced the length of the chamber muttering to himself, Knox palmed the pulse thumping in his belly, willing himself to breathe through his momentary jolt of panic. He had to wed at some point. Men attached themselves to women they didn't love for economic purposes every day. Birthrights were routinely salvaged by juicy settlements. Marrying for love was uncommon, even considered odd. That two of the three DeWitts had found wives they cherished was a miracle.

With his responsibilities, Knox couldn't hold out hope for miracles.

However...that kiss in a dimly lit millinery had taken hold and wasn't letting go. He'd lain in bed the past three nights bandying it about in his head like a cricket ball. Certainly, he'd desired Clarissa Marlowe since the first day he'd seen her. No one would argue this. One look across her scarred counter, and he'd been knocked from his feet. But those had been a smitten man's dreams, far from reach. Now, after he'd gone and touched her...

If only she hadn't mentioned he had *competition*.

Exhaling softly, Knox tilted his head to glance at the dripping sconce on the wall that needed repair. Like much of this ducal manor, it craved attention. Attention requiring funds. What he felt for his gorgeous milliner was lust, not a practical circumstance for a man with five ailing estates to manage. Not to mention the villages, tenants, and staff attached. Knox had hundreds of souls dependent upon him. He couldn't let his aching cock make a decision about such a weighty matter.

Even if he did feel the utmost serenity of his life every time he stepped into her shop. The way he imagined he'd feel upon returning from the House of Lords to his waiting duchess.

He knew, without doubt, that Clarissa Marlowe would slam the door in his face should he ask her to be his mistress. A brief affair, she might agree to. Being owned, she would not.

Anyway, a man who loved his mistress but not his wife was asking for the worst kind of strife.

"This list is bollocks," Cort said as he stopped by the sideboard. Pouring himself a drink, he slammed the whisky back, then wiped his lips with his wrist. He waved the sheet in the air like a flag. "There isn't one chit here I'd agree to. Not one."

Knox picked up his quill and drew lazy circles on his ledger to keep his temper in check. He should have known better than to ask a man so besotted with his wife that he wouldn't leave her for even one night to confer on this mess. "Thankfully, you don't have to agree, brother of mine. What about Helena Parker-Mantling? She's quite nice and has spent three seasons dodging suitors from the looks of it. She whipped me in an archery match last year, strongest arm on the girl of any I've seen in England. Her father has given me clear signals about her availability."

Damien chimed in from his spot by the bookcase. "Rumor is she's besotted with the lead in the latest Drury Lane production," he said, flipping pages. "I saw her backstage when I was visiting with Mercy last week. I'd go in another direction if I were you."

This was credible information as Damien's wife was the theatre's artist in residence.

"Female or male lead?" Cort asked, the beginnings of a grin curving his lips.

Damien coughed politely into his pages. "I'd rather not say."

Slamming his glass to the sideboard, Cort marched to Knox's desk, slipped the quill from his hand, and struck a line through Lady Parker-Mantling's name.

Knox scowled. His brother often acted like he was still on a battlefield, ordering everyone about like a colonel.

Damien strolled over, his shadow falling across them. Somewhere along the way, he'd gotten taller than both his brothers. "Who else do you have there? The leading candidate, that is."

Knox closed his ledger before his brothers got close enough to read the dismal figures and slipped it into a drawer. "Baroness Barclay, I suppose."

Cort shook his head, striking through her name as well.

Knox came out of his chair, grabbing for the list. Cort backed up, holding it out of reach. "Why reject her? She comes from a respected family. Her husband has been gone long enough for a wedding to create absolutely no scandal. A bit sour in the face, but she's lively and—"

"I had, um, a brief association with her before I found Alex again." Cort glanced around the study, avoiding his brother's gazes. "Let's leave it at that. And please never mention this to my wife, will you? She doesn't take kindly to my indiscretions, even if she was married then, and I was heartsick about it."

"Can't have that kind of tension at family gatherings and such, I agree," Damien murmured, snatching the list free of Cort's hand. "Alexandra DeWitt can be frightening when she's vexed. We've all seen it. The last time I irritated her, she raced one of those demon horses of hers right at me. I had to dive into the hedges to escape."

Knox swore and tumbled back into his chair. "Couldn't keep your trousers buttoned, could you?"

Cort snorted and headed back to the sideboard. "You're not one to talk, Your Grace."

"Anyone you've sampled on the list, Dame?" Knox highly doubted there was, but he might as well ask. Several years ago, after an evening of carousing, his youngest brother had told him that although he'd done many things with many women, he'd never *bedded* one. Shocked wasn't a strong enough word for his response at hearing this news. Evidently, the Troublesome Trio weren't as troublesome as presumed.

Damien reviewed the list, grimaced, then wres-

boots. He'd defeated that nitwit Clarence with that exhilarating kiss.

"Another bonnet?" Damien asked, puzzled. "We've got too many already. Mercy said I can't bring another, not one, into the house. You'll have to go to the streets to find a recipient."

"*Christ*," Cort said, "you are the most green lad in this city, Damien DeWitt."

Knox turned to his brothers, his grin beatific. Happiness was a bright light at the end of a dark, ducal tunnel. "Oh, no, this is the most magnificent bonnet yet. And it's all for *me*."

Clarissa was nervous, an uncommon occurrence.

Her strained childhood had been the best training in the world for overcoming unease about one's circumstances. She'd learned to display a calm façade while her guts were churning. She'd cast up her accounts more times than she could remember after those dreaded trips to her father's manse. In the carriage, outside the carriage, on the marble steps of his home. So much so, that her mother had taken to carrying a basket with them on each visit.

Lost in the past, Clarissa dawdled with the knight on her chess board. If she moved it to g5, she could potentially attack both the queen *and* the bishop. She brought the piece close to her face and turned it over, reading the artist's initials carved into the base. Her father had given her the set on her twelfth birthday. It was at least two hundred years old and worth a small fortune.

And held the honor of being one of the few things she'd refused to allow her mother to sell when the shop was close to going under.

Clarissa adored chess, even if she loathed the man who'd inspired her to play the game.

She glanced to the window, as she had every minute since sending her impromptu note to a duke. It was snowing steadily, a lovely layer of pearl lining the sill. He likely wouldn't consider accepting a decree under such circumstances. Carriages overturned all the time on days like these. Important men didn't travel in squalls. She'd sent her staff of two home earlier, citing the storm when a potential guest was the true reason. She couldn't afford live-in domestics, only day help, so this wasn't truly a bother.

Besides, he had women who would come to *him*. Why, Lady Dowling had fainted in his arms last week, according to the gossip rags.

Aggrieved, she plunked the knight to the board with a thump. She'd made the Duke of Herschel work too hard for her appreciation. Teased him for too long that evening in her shop. Peers of the realm didn't take to playfulness. They preferred domination over every female they encountered, the brutes.

However...

Clarissa picked up the queen and rotated the gorgeous ivory piece in her hand. Knoxville DeWitt had a gentle side. He loved his brothers to distraction. Part of the reason she'd let him purchase bonnets when she knew he didn't *need* another bonnet was the sweetness of the Troublesome Trio's visits.

He stood close to his siblings, vigilant, almost looming. Especially the younger brother, Damien. If they weren't with him, he *talked* about them. And their wives. And their children. Incessantly. It was clear to her that the man loved his family—and desired his own.

She decided she would go to Bath for a respite

when he selected his duchess. The broadsheets would be filled with the exploits of a duke and his lady love.

Clarissa wasn't a woman who embraced heartache.

The knock on the front door echoed down her hallway. She stood and gave her home a last, lingering review, wondering what her personal effects said about her. Her residence in Clerkenwell was modest but pleasant. And it was *hers*, paid for with revenue from her profession. She'd considered looking at more prosperous districts when she'd bought this cottage outright two years ago, but she loved it. So, here she stayed.

Thankfully, aside from the chess board, there wasn't a hint of her father about.

Or her mother, for that matter.

Clarissa took a deep breath and smoothed her hand over her chignon and down her bodice. Her legs were unsteady but hidden by rose silk the color of a vibrant sunrise. Her modiste was the best in Clerkenwell, and she didn't wear these gowns while working.

They were for her.

And maybe, just maybe, for the man she would invite to know more.

She expected a liveried footman to be looming on her portico when she opened the door, announcing her titled guest. And from the bewildered look on his handsome face, the duke expected to see a housekeeper. Snow fluttered past and into the entryway as they stared, but the chill was extinguished by the simmer bubbling beneath her skin. His gaze lowered to her feet, then slowly rose to her face. He held one of his elegant beaver hats in his gloved hand. (She knew the maker, the finest in London.) His dark gray greatcoat was open as if he'd thrown it on and raced from his Mayfair terrace. His waistcoat was a buttery hue somewhere close to the color of the cream the local grocer delivered each morning. His cravat was a simple coil, per his style. She appreciated the elegant simplicity of his dress.

Still, his jaw was stubbled, his cheeks flushed, his magnificent lips pursed, the bottom caught between his straight, white teeth. Teeth she'd grazed with her tongue three short days ago. And those eyes of his struck deep, stark sea green against the winter mist surrounding him.

*My*, she thought and clenched her hand in her skirt.

Whether she approved of this or not, she was smitten.

Attracted. In want…yearning…*need*.

And he was here. Apparently, he felt the same.

This understanding gave Clarissa the courage to step back and usher the Duke of Herschel into her private life.

Into her inner sanctum.

If he realized what a feat this was, he would have been astonished.

Wordless, he followed her down the narrow corridor to the parlor. The only one in the house. It was cozy, the hearthfire roaring, souchong tea in a pot on the table scented the air. Trying to disregard the sense of him standing so close, she procured his coat and hat, watching in suppressed awe as he removed his gloves with his teeth. With a hard swallow, she hung up the garments while he gazed about her home, cataloging, his expression bemused, curious. There was a mix of scoundrel and nobleman about him that intrigued her beyond measure.

Knoxville DeWitt had rough edges she wished to explore.

She'd never found anyone without them interesting in the least.

Also, she liked, *loved*, that he gave her time. He was patient. He didn't push. He teased, unequivocally, but never pushed. In her experience, men often pressured a woman until she had her back to the wall. Clarissa only wanted her back to the wall if a duke's lips were covering hers while he did the pressing.

"What's that sly smile about?" he asked, settling himself on the only article in the room that would hold him, a Gillows armchair she'd purchased from a baron who'd gambled his fortune away. She'd obtained several of his pieces after his wife had come into her shop asking to resell her bonnets to pay their monthly coal bill.

Clarissa dashed her hand over her cheek while her back was turned, willing away the heat. It wouldn't do to let him see too much. Radical honesty wasn't a part of this bargain.

"Maybe I'm surprised you showed up in this weather." She crossed to the sofa, the table acting as a chaperone between them. Sitting, she poured from the tea pot with an elegance that possibly surprised him. Although she wasn't a lady, for a time, she'd been educated like one. "I sent my staff home, so I'm alone. There are only two during the day, in any case, nothing like the legions you employ."

With a shiver, he accepted the cup, wrapping his slim fingers around the bone china. "A damned blizzard couldn't have kept me away, Miss Marlowe. Furthermore, I'm delighted to find that we're alone."

She glanced to the window, discomfited by his candor. He tended to do that. Speak his mind without worry. *It must be nice*, she thought. Women were never allowed such liberties. "I think a blizzard is what you're getting."

hot, his body hard. "I'll agree to your demands." Pausing, he gently bit her neck, then laved the stinging spot with his tongue. For the first time in her life, she almost swooned. "If you'll consider my suggestions, Miss Marlowe."

She shook her head, but instead of pulling away —*damn him*—she nestled closer. She held as still as possible as it was impossible to ignore the effect she was having on him. His shaft was a rigid, tempting presence against her bottom. "I'm listening," she finally whispered.

With a nudge of his cheek against hers, he directed her gaze to the window. The bottom panes were almost completely covered in white. "I suggest we begin our association *today*, not in the near future. I don't have anywhere to be until Thursday afternoon, which gives us a full twenty hours for play."

"*Play*," she breathed, having no idea what this meant.

"*Pleasure*." He kissed her earlobe, sucking the sliver of skin between his lips. Her heart dropped as a shiver raced through her. "Consider this an introduction. We'll enjoy each other without going the full measure. Then, I'll leave for my appointment and you to manage your shop, with plans to return here as soon as I can manage it. *If* you decide you'd like to continue. The decision will be entirely yours." He kissed his way down her neck, halting at the filigree border of her gown. "I only ask that you please, *please*, call me Knox. Or arrogant cur, if it suits. 'Your Grace' is absent in this place. I'm a man in Clerkenwell, not a bloody duke."

Her mind churned with possibilities. His fortitude apparently encompassed his lovemaking as well. *It's no wonder the Duke of Herschel is sought after*, she thought, dazed. She shrugged a shoulder. "I don't know how to play."

Knox turned her in his arms, walking her back until she bumped the escritoire in the corner of her parlor. His mouth covered hers as he placed her atop its thankfully empty surface. "I'll teach you. Lessons in love for lessons in chess," he murmured against her lips before he took her under.

# CHAPTER 3

## WHERE A DUKE ENTERS ANOTHER WORLD

*H*e'd never negotiated with a woman to secure an assignation.

One benefit of the title, he supposed.

Nevertheless, Clarissa Marlowe, standing in the doorway of her charming cottage, a gown the hue of week-old red roses swimming down her slender body, her expression bold and scared witless at the same time, had done something to him. A weak-kneed something.

A violent twist to his heart—when he'd scurried to Clerkenwell for twists to be done to his cock.

Desiring to protect as urgently as he desired to seduce was a rather novel sensation.

And, *ah, hell,* did he want her.

Aching, blinding need. Groundswells of yearning he hadn't confronted in this lifetime.

Knox thought it rather generous that he'd offered to delay taking her to bed when he'd dreamed of that blessedly divine event for *months*. Getting a glimpse of her pleasure, in any manner, would be enough for now. He hoped.

When he stepped between her legs, spreading them as much as her skirt allowed, she welcomed him by parting her lips beneath his. He tilted her head just so, wanting this to last for eons, a piece of the puzzle he'd often hurried through. She was quite the best kisser, amazing when he suspected she'd not had much opportunity to practice.

Some things, he guessed, merely *were*.

She'd better not have learned from that dolt Clarence.

Fearlessly, she circled her tongue around his, urging him into *her* rhythm—a dance, a race, an age-old battle. She tasted of tea and the faint hint of cinnamon, and he was lost. They fell into a sensual abyss, sending the ground shifting beneath his feet. He groaned and cradled her jaw, possessing, seeking all she would give. Her breasts were a plump delight against his chest, her hands resting on his shoulders, one rising to seek out the hair at the nape of his neck. To coil the strands and scrape his scalp. Her breath streaked down his throat, her sighs mixing with the slight rise of her body to reach him.

*How would it be*, he marveled, *when she was beneath him, astride him, gazing over her shoulder as he pleasured her from behind?*

He struggled to contain his enthusiasm at the visions.

Impatient, he lifted her exquisite gown and thin chemise—a shocking surprise, the frock, when she'd answered her door looking like a goddess—in fistfuls until he had more clearance to settle between her legs. He desperately longed to nestle his cock against her supple folds while making her cry out in ecstasy.

When he'd promised an introduction, he meant a thorough one.

The kiss got away from him, as the impromptu match in her shop had, and he forgot his place, his plan. His fingers tunneled through her hair, pins slipping to the floor, her chignon tumbling free, before he remembered he was taking this slowly.

She flinched, putting space between them, reaching for her disheveled twist. "*Knox.*"

He tipped her chin until her gaze met his. Her eyes were a dewy, smoky gray, inviting him to ruin her. To ruin himself. "There you go, love. At last, my name on your delicious lips."

She let a streaking sigh whisper free, her arms falling to her side. "Is this play?"

He hesitated, understanding the precipice he stood upon. A gaping, thunderous next step loomed before them. She had no idea how much her awakening would change her. How much inducing her awakening could change *him*. "No, love, it isn't play. Not the kind I had in mind, in any case. Although it's amazingly perfect this marvelous, astounding kiss, if that's all we ever do."

"If I agree, play is as far as it goes this day?" She patted her chest, drawing his eyes to the breasts rounding out her bodice most pleasingly. He couldn't wait to tease her pert nipples until she was breathless with need, should he be allowed the honor. "The rest will truly be my choice?"

He shoved aside his brief irritation that she would think she didn't have sovereignty over their rendezvous. Over her decision *or* her body. Then he recalled the restrictions placed on women in their world. They didn't choose their husbands or manage their own finances. They couldn't vote or voice opinions without being ostracized. Clarissa Marlowe was as independent as any chit he'd ever come across—and he'd best remember this if he wanted to keep her for even one second.

Pressing his lips tenderly to hers, he curled his hand around her waist and brought her against him.

He leaned to kiss her knee, trailing his mouth along her thigh. Her skin was as soft as the stockings he held. Her intimate fragrance was doing wondrous things to his heartbeat, the thump of blood pulsing through his veins. He'd never been lightheaded before, the beauty of the act rendering him speechless.

Pushing past the unfamiliar feeling of trepidation, he cupped her bottom, and pulled her against his mouth, slicking his tongue across her folds. Her stockings tumbled to the floor. In the most erotic move in his memory, she arched into the contact, offering herself to him, bumping her pelvis against his cheek.

"*Touch me*," she murmured thickly, sending his arousal careening so high he was puzzled at being able to remain on his feet. The punch of pleasure had him groaning against her, flicking his tongue across the knot of nerves topping her sex. In reply to the vibration, she tunneled her hands through his hair and whimpered. Not a shout...merely a raw, unbidden *whimper*.

He'd never heard a sound as primally blissful.

The rest of the campaign to bring her to orgasm was a blur. His chest hitching, his heartbeat pulsing in his ears, he endeavored to memorize every crease, curl, and fold. Every delicate valley and exquisite ridge. She tasted of ambrosia, nectar of the gods. *Go gently, Knox*, he advised himself. However, his mouth was intent, tongue seeking, lips molding around her while her juices flowed, both of them too committed to pleasure to dally.

He longed to sample when instead he feasted.

The sounds echoing about the parlor were comprised of her coarse demands and his responding murmurs of approval. His own skin was moist, his shirt sticking to his back. He wanted the garments on both of them *gone*. A considerable part of him wished he'd never offered to play. *Fucking idiot*. When he wanted to shove her back, wrap her slender legs around his waist, and sink his hard length inside her. Pump and grind until neither of them could walk. *For days.*

Knowing he'd about reached his limit, his cock near to bursting, he trailed his fingers along her silken folds and teased at her entrance. While she emitted these husky little sounds again, he worked one finger, then two, into her sleek channel. She slumped to her elbows, her head falling back, the crown nearly touching the desk.

"*Knox*," was all she whispered in a gravelly voice.

Maddened, his lips closed around the rigid nub controlling her release as his fingers brought her to a frenzy. He grasped her hip with his free hand to hold her in place, wringing every bit of pleasure from the moment. He wasn't especially proud of the fact that he knew he could make her come in seconds, maybe a minute. Nor was he proud of the fact that she'd almost made him spend in his drawers like a wee lad.

When he fucked her the first time, his life would be complete.

Of course, Clarissa worsened his arousal by looping her slender leg over his shoulder, bringing him in and under her, his fingers driving, his tongue and lips consuming. There were no times before her, before *this*. The past vanished.

His mind was an absolute blank aside from her.

He'd never been torn apart by a female before.

Her fingers tightened in his hair as her hips lifted. She shuddered, quivers racing along her arms and legs. He looked up in time to catch the bowing of her body, her hand grasping the desk, her knuckles as pale as the snow falling outside. Her cries rippled through the air, charging the space until her heat was greater than the blaze radiating from the hearthfire.

At the last, she shoved him away with a gasp, sliding off the desk, and to her knees before him, her skirts fluttering about before settling in a crumpled puddle at her feet. Stunned, she palmed the floor with one hand, her body shaking. Her hair was a shroud hanging over her face and past her shoulders. Her chest rose on staggered gasps, the only noise in the room aside from the splintering wood in the grate.

Knox started to apologize but words were lost to him. Perhaps he'd been too rough. Too hasty, using everything he'd learned when a minute percentage would have sufficed for an introductory session. Truthfully, once he'd gotten a look at her, a goddess spilled across the desk, ivory hair and glistening skin, what choice had he had? Was it his fault he'd raced outside his normal, controlled parameters in pursuit of pleasure?

When he longed to do things to this woman *he'd* never dared do with another. Secret fantasies involving cravats, bedposts, blindfolds, and seduction. Cursing softly, he shook himself free of his carnal absorption. *Bloody hell*, he decided, he'd been too energetic with an inexperienced partner. He would tread more carefully next time.

If his gorgeous milliner consented to another rendezvous after this.

Clarissa glanced through the dense, flaxen cloak. Her eyes were the color of pewter, the lids hooded in half-arousal. She licked her lips, her purr one of utter delight. "Your turn, Your Grace."

Knox frowned in confusion as his cock roared to life, straining against his trouser close. Staggered, he rocked back on his heels. "But, you..." Gesturing inanely, he scrubbed a bead of sweat from his temple. "You were, I was too, that is—"

"*Shh.*" She crawled to him on her hands and knees, a bloody dream if there ever was one. "You were too *everything*. And it's been the most extraordinary afternoon of my recollection." Halting before him, she pressed her mouth to his, her lips open, pulling him into a kiss that had *him* palming the floor to steady himself. "So, that's what I taste like," she whispered and drew back enough to stare into his eyes.

Her smile was feral, the sated flush staining her cheeks telling a lewd story.

His heart caught, his groan streaking free. He hadn't hurt her. He'd shown her the untamed man, not the guarded duke, and she'd liked it. Liked *him*.

"Where have you been all my life, Clarissa Marlowe?"

She ran her tongue over her teeth, toying with him. "At the Petal and Plume on Bond Street, Your Grace. I started assisting in the shop when I was seven, in fact."

He frowned, truly puzzled, and so aroused, that crouching in this position was fast becoming an impossibility. He flexed his fingers, the piquant aroma of her drifting past his nose. It was a crude gesture, but she caught his meaning. "I didn't hurt you?"

She laughed and trailed her knuckle down his waistcoat, circling each button. "I have a device. Wood covered in boiled leather. The same kind used to make armor. It readied me, I suppose, for this. I found a shop in Shoreditch that sells unique items."

He about swallowed his tongue. "*Device?*"

Her gaze lowered to his crotch and the cock straining for release. "It was advertised as a gadget resembling the virile male member. I believe, from fur-

working its way up his spine meaning he had little time left.

"Soon, love," he gasped, his fingertips pressing into her scalp. "Soon."

She didn't sit back or slow down. *Oh, no*, she became more intent on her mission.

When she began to hum, her tongue wrapping around his shaft, he forgot all sense of decorum and cried out, his hips rising. The orgasm ripped through him, dimming his vision, and taking his breath. He removed himself from her care with only seconds to spare, shooting his seed across the linen shirt wadded around his belly as fierce sensations conquered him. In the end, when she blew a breath of air across his bullocks, he suspected he'd entered heaven.

Slumping back, he tossed his arm across his eyes in submission. Whatever stunned expression sat on his face, she didn't need to see.

A panting, erotic display of a man at his weakest. They hadn't thought to extinguish so much as one lamp.

It was, though he'd never admit it, the quickest he'd ever come from a bout of oral consideration in all his days.

Seconds ticked by on a clock somewhere in the room. The wind slapped the panes in a howling roar. The hearthfire crackled, wood shifting in the grate. He drew a lungful of the stimulating flavor of *them*. As reason returned, Knox heard Clarissa arranging her clothing, her breathing slowing to match his. She'd been excited, too, to the point of noticeability. In his experience, not many women liked this part of the act, while most men *loved* it.

Clarissa Marlowe was unique in ways he'd not imagined. He only had to figure out what to do about her.

When he heard a hinge squeak, Knox lifted his arm to find Clarissa in the doorway, a bemused smile curving her lips. Hair wild, cheeks rosy, gown ruined, she looked spectacularly undone. Yet, in control of her faculties, which made *one* of them.

No one should be in such capable management of their body and mind after *this*.

"I fear you may be here longer than you'd planned. The snow is already knee-high and falling faster. The streets are impossible to navigate, from what I can tell."

He merely grunted, exhausted to his bones, and still thinking about how quickly he'd come. Her talent was humbling.

Hiding her amusement without success, she tipped her shoulder to the back of the cottage and gave a lazy shrug. "I'm going to gather foodstuff. I'll be back. Don't get up." Then, impossibly, daringly, fucking brilliantly, she laughed. "I find the afternoon's activities have made me simply ravenous."

## CHAPTER 4

### WHERE A DETERMINED WOMAN
### UNLOCKS A SECRET OR TWO

*M*ercifully, the Duke of Herschel was skilled at lovemaking, because he was horrid at chess.

Clarissa sighed as Knox placed his pawn directly in front of her king, creating all kinds of vulnerabilities for his campaign. He peered at her across the board, his expression charmingly tentative. Stalling for time, he gave his signet ring a twist. His eyes had calmed to a mellow apple-green, though they glowed beautifully in the lamplight. When she'd returned, she'd made a cozy spot for them before the fire, where they sat, cross-legged and half-dressed, casual as could be. Thirty-two ivory pieces all that was resting between them. "That move made it worse, didn't it? You're going to sweep in again, three in a bloody row I've lost. I feel deceived by your extreme proficiency. In many areas."

She pressed her lips together to hide her smile, watching him tear into his meat pie with a growl. The man hated to lose, and she was loathe to tell him, but he would never beat her at this game. He was talented—*oh, so, talented*—but not at chess.

Moreover, because he seemed a little touchy

about 'arriving' so quickly during their play, she was hesitant to defeat him outright.

She took a sip of ale, a rare treat from the brewer down the street. The duke's raised brows when she'd served the drink had been another reminder of the difference in their stations. No society miss served a guest beer. Certainly not a duke. She was sorry, but she didn't have champagne. Or whisky, his favorite according to him.

Nonetheless, Clarissa relished the bubble at the back of her throat and the faint buzz in her brain. Although Knox didn't know it, she was struggling to keep from reaching for him, dragging him to the floor, and finding out how many other ways he could make her *come*. His word, new to her, and a polite way of describing the mind-altering sensation of leaving one's body. She could still feel tremors zipping along her back and buttocks. She was tender and swollen, wet between her thighs. She could taste him if she tried very hard to, and the look on his face as he climaxed would be burned into her memory forevermore. There'd been nothing remotely highbrow about any of it. Both of them a sweaty, gasping, wonder.

Alley or ballroom, lust was lust.

Why, somewhere in the middle of his onslaught, he'd murmured that he had a *thousand* ways to pleasure her. Whispers of silk cravats and wrists tied to bedposts, she'd been awash in excitement.

She wanted each of the nine hundred and ninety-nine ways to be *hers*.

Although they'd never have enough time for that. He'd be married, his duchess giving him the family she knew he wanted long before they could muscle through even fifty orgasms.

The thought sent a dull pang through her.

"Tell me something," he said around a bite of cheese, possibly to draw her back into the room and away from her second's grief. Possibly to keep from making another dreadful decision in their game. "I'm curious. Where did you come upon this chess set? The Spode teacups? They seem...out of place in Clerkenwell, if that isn't too forward a statement."

Clarissa leaned against the wall, stretching her legs, and wiggling her bare toes before the fire. Knox's gaze hungrily tracked the movement, sending a thrill through her. He'd done away with his boots and waistcoat. His sleeves were rolled past the elbow, exposing his muscular forearms and a light dusting of dark hair. It was the height of intimacy for a girl who'd never invited a man into her home, aside from the fact that she'd recently taken lewd liberties with his person. A dimly lit parlor, the scent of sex riding her skin, her stockings in a crumpled wad by her new lover's hip, her taste on *his* tongue. Not to mention the stains on his shirt he'd tried to remove while she made them a repast of cheese, meat pies, and slices of seed cake from the baker next door.

"You're prying, Your Grace," she said, though she smiled to show she wasn't offended in the least. She was curious about him as well. If she answered his questions, he would have to answer hers.

He bowed his head, for a moment the titled topper he was. "I apologize."

She recalled that he'd very kindly stated, during an intense moment when he was suckling her thigh, that he wanted to know her outside the sensual part.

Fiddling with her rook, Clarissa traced the crenellations notched in ivory that made it resemble a medieval castle. It was her favorite piece. "I came by the set and the teacups and a few other things by way of my father. He routinely gave me lavish gifts rather than spend an afternoon in the park with me. Ice cream at Gunter's would have meant more. His attention was saved for his legitimate children, or so I've heard." She popped the rook in place with more displeasure than she wished to exhibit. "He shared his love of chess, and for that, if nothing else, I thank him. Too, he never lied to my mother about what he *wasn't* prepared to do, which was publicly acknowledge me. Privately, he patted me on the head and called me darling daughter."

Knox paused, words backing up in his throat. She could see him combing through them, deciding on the best approach.

"I'll stop you before you ask. Ernest Lehigh Danes, Viscount Pemberly."

Knox choked on his cheese and coughed into his fist. Rolling her eyes, Clarissa scooted his mug closer with her foot. He drank liberally, then wiped his lips with his wrist. "Holy hell, you're not joking. *That's* why you have the grace of a duchess, the speech of a queen. Pemberly, eh? He's a member at White's. Cheats at cards, they say. Among other indiscretions."

Clarissa nibbled on a slice of cake, in slight disbelief. Knoxville DeWitt was the first person she'd ever told about her father. "He has a rather dreadful reputation, and trust me, it's deserved. He made promises to my mother, left her, then returned to make more. For years. Kept her from marrying anyone else when she had decent offers because she was always pining for him. Even after he wed, he wouldn't let her go. She couldn't face the truth of her situation, that titled men don't marry milliners. Although he provided the occasional governess when he was feeling generous, hence my seemingly adequate schooling. Watching them battle my entire childhood made me want nothing *less* than to be committed in that way. They made each other miserable."

The Duke of Herschel wanted to dispute her assertion about a union between his class and hers, but he could not. "You think she should have kissed the viscount goodbye."

Clarissa chewed furiously and swallowed hard. Yes, she did. Now, she'd gone and involved herself with a blasted duke and worried she'd have trouble kissing *him* goodbye.

Knox gestured her way with a hunk of bread. "I don't think I like that look," he said around a bite. "I'm no Pemberly. Here, in this lovely cottage, we agreed, I'm *nothing*. Just a man who wants you more than he can convey with mere words. I left the duke dilemma on the doorstep."

She tossed back a gulp of beer, the warmth in her belly soothing her. "Lady Dowling might disagree. She thinks you're something."

"Enough of this. You're getting foxed." Knox reached for her glass, wiggling it from her fingers. "I don't even know the chit. It's not as if I could let her tumble to the marble slabs, could I?"

Clarissa slumped back, a bit dizzy, guessing the ale was getting to her. As was the sight of her duke sprawled across the faded Aubusson she'd bought from a down-on-his-luck baron. His legs crossed at the ankle, his thighs shifting with each move he made, those long, slim fingers he'd thrust inside her picking apart a piece of cake. She knew what lay beneath his trouser buttons, knew the taste and feel of him well enough to sketch him. He had to be the most attractive man in England, he just *had* to be. And for a few more hours, he was hers. "Dukes have to be heroes. I understand. It's in your blood."

"Not like your young Clarence, maker of shoes.

An honest lad, I'm sure. Never caught a girl on her way down."

Laughter bubbled from deep in her throat. "He kisses like a fish."

Knox slapped his glass to the floor, a curse shooting from between his teeth. "You bloody kissed him after what we shared in your shop?"

"I had to." Clarissa released an exaggerated sigh, fanning her face for effect. "Fair is fair. Don't look so displeased. You won the contest." Of course, she hadn't kissed Clarence. But there was no reason to let this arrogant toad have the upper hand when he'd bedded half the women in London.

He opened his mouth to quarrel, then closed it with a snap. His gaze when it circled back to her was a burning emerald blaze. "I'm so bloody possessive of you, in a way I've never been. I yearn for you. Your taste, your touch. Quiet conversations in that damned shop of yours. I don't keep mistresses, no matter what you think of me. My nights are becoming quite tame as the Troublesome Trio is no more. I'm the only man standing. You are the woman I want yet—"

"You must marry."

"It's more than merely having to supply the next male in the DeWitt line." He dropped his head to his hand and massaged his brow. "Not to go on about it, but my father was a brute with a title and grand expectations for his sons, especially his heir. I spent my youth protecting Damien and Cort, leaving myself exposed to his brutality. In addition to a ghastly nature, he managed money poorly. He left the duchy in a dire situation, the coffers lighter than a feather. To be blunt, I can't go on much longer without an infusion of cash."

*Oh*, she thought, *this is it.* Her heart ached for him

—and for herself. They had no chance. "You need a plum settlement."

He glanced up, his face a mask of misery. "I have nearly a thousand people under my care, love. Tenants who need firewood, food, and medical care. Roads in one village are a disaster, and a church's roof in another is close to caving in. Staff, children of staff, animals, elders, estates bound to me until I breathe my last. Five of them at last count. My options are becoming rather limited. Noose around my neck limited. I had a small emergency fund built up last year, but I let Damien have it for his marriage, and I'm incredibly glad I did."

Pushing to his feet, he crossed to the window, nudging the curtain aside to gaze into the late afternoon mist. Despair lay heavy upon his broad shoulders, it was plain to see. Snow was falling madly, the roads impassable at this point. No one would be coming to her shop until the weather cleared. Her customers would know why it was closed.

Clarissa pressed her hand to her heart. She wanted Knox to stay a little longer. Another day. Perhaps two.

Then, she *would* kiss the duke goodbye.

She crossed to him, making no effort to hide her step. His shoulders tensed, but otherwise, Knox held his stance. "I'm sorry if the play got out of hand," he murmured, his gaze still fixed on the wintry scene outside the window. "I lost myself somewhere along the way. I know we had an agreement. I don't mean to break it."

Emotion overcoming her, she wrapped her arms around him, resting her cheek on his back. She wanted to shield him, the most protective sensation she'd ever felt. "Can you stay until the storm clears?"

He turned, keeping her in his arms. His emerald

Time.

He meant to take it.

Halting her, Knox pulled her into an embrace not far from one he'd employ if dancing the waltz. The kiss was light, her lips opening beneath his in surprise, then passion. He backed her into the wall, running his hands from her shoulders to her waist before tucking her tightly against him. "I love kissing you," he murmured against the corner of her mouth, "when I've never appreciated the act this much. You are divine in every sense."

She nipped his bottom lip, launching air in a spiral through his lungs. "You were in a hurry for other things, Your Grace."

He cradled her cheek, watching her steely eyes glaze and glisten. "There isn't anyone else. Not in my heart or my mind. It's as if you've magically erased my past. I..." He halted, unsure how to tell her without telling her too much when she still meant to kiss a duke goodbye.

Falling in love with Clarissa Marlowe would be a very cruel thing, indeed.

As if she knew what he was thinking, she took his hand and led him to a door at the end of the hallway. If he'd known nothing about her, this room would have told all. It smelled of lilies and hyacinth, the fragrances he'd often caught on her skin. Moonlit and nothing but lit the chamber, revealing bonnets in various stages of completion scattered about the space. It wasn't messy so much as spirited, like the woman. The curtains were without frills, the furniture sedate and steady, but the vases lining a shelf were splashes of color.

The bed was the most inviting he'd ever seen. Stacked with pillows, rose-colored silk draped over the tester frame like moss, the counterpane a darker shade of crimson, bold and elegant.

He paused in the doorway, where she glanced at him over her shoulder.

It was true. He was nervous. This slip of a woman had a lofty duke twisted in a knot. Because she was revealing more than he'd ever been given. "No one but you is allowed in here, am I right, love?"

In response, she grasped his shirt in her hand and dragged him inside her chamber. Sank her fingers into the hair riding the nape of his neck and pulled him into a kiss he wasn't sure he'd survive.

It was answer enough.

They walked each other toward the bed, circling, kissing, moaning. Their own brand of the waltz. Her breast was full and plump, his thumb teasing her peaked nipple through layers. His first touch of this part of her body. He was going to suck them. *Soon*. Bite and lick and *savor*. Her waist was gently curved, perfect for his hold. Hip to hip, they bumped, grinding against each other until he was hard and she ready. Breathless, she took command, turning so it was his legs that met the edge of the mattress, where he tumbled. Grabbing her, he laughed, pulling her atop him.

The subsequent struggle was fun *and* sensual, novel in his experience.

She unbuttoned his shirt with remarkable speed without breaking the kiss, shoving it from his shoulders in triumph like she'd raised a flag on a ship she'd captured. His trousers and drawers were rolled off in awkward twists and rotations between puffs of amusement. When he encountered trouble disrobing *her*, she rose to her knees, presenting her back to him. He worked past ties and hooks, nibbling on each slice of skin he revealed through a chemise as silky and transparent as gossamer. In seconds, both garments fluttered to the floor.

"*Stop*," Knox whispered when she made to turn, releasing a tight breath across her bare skin.

She glanced back uncertainly, her bottom lip caught between her teeth. Her ardent gaze swept the length of him, lingering in a sensual way that lit him up inside.

"I want to look. A minute pause before I lose my mind in pleasure."

In acceptance, her chin dipped, allowing him his wish.

She was slender, and shapely, her skin the color of fresh cream. Her hair was a tousled tumble of gold. Smiling, he traced the light dusting of freckles along the slope of her shoulders and over her pert bottom. He trailed his hand between her cheeks and through the thatch of hair still damp from their earlier adventure. With a moan, she collapsed, bracing her arms on the mattress as he gently tunneled his finger inside her. He leaned over her, curving his body around hers as he thrust. "Someday, will you let me watch you use your toy? I want to see you come by your own method."

He didn't expect an answer, as this was a fantasy. *Every* man's fantasy. And those rarely came true. Except, Clarissa Marlowe was unique to the extreme. "If you let me…watch you," she whispered in a husky voice and reared back to drive his fingers deeper.

Her answer and her pursuit unleashed a demon inside him.

Tilting her head, Knox kissed her, bringing her back into the storm. He worked his arm beneath her to cushion the fall as he turned her to her back and laid his body over hers. There were no instructions, no guidance from either party. It was instinctive sport. His hips sank between her open thighs, her arms looping over his shoulders, mouths fusing, tongues meeting and drawing each other in.

They explored in full measure. The globes of her breast cupped in his hand, her nipple hardening as he suckled, his tongue swirling. Her fingers circled his cock and stroked. Hip to hip, they broke into a rhythm predicting things to come. She was a wildfire, rising to meet his touch, whispering about how he was making her feel, what she wanted to do to him. He'd never been with a woman who held *nothing* back.

It was extraordinary.

Anchoring her knee by his hip, she opened herself to him. Biting his neck, she murmured, "Now, Knox, *now.*"

He couldn't deny her. She was ready, her folds wet and swollen. As for him, he'd been gone for her for months, maybe longer. His cock wanted no other home.

Sweeping her hair from her eyes, he stared into them as he worked his shaft into place. "I desire you more than I've desired anyone in my life, Clarissa Marlowe. You understand that, don't you?"

Before she could respond, he thrust gently, working his way inside her. She was tight but not uncomfortably so. He fit her nipple between his lips, mouthing the side of her breast, dragging her attention away from any discomfort below. Arching her back with a ragged groan, she brought her other leg around him, her heel digging into his buttock, sending him deeper. And deeper still. A moment's hesitation and her slight cry was the only moment she stilled. Then they were moving together, halting at first, before the pace settled into a steady pace.

The kiss was uncontrolled, out of rhythm with his

## CHAPTER 6

WHERE A LOVE-STRUCK MILLINER
MAKES A DECISION

Clarissa glanced up as the door to her shop opened, her heart dropping to see it wasn't the Duke of Herschel.

*Knox*. Now, she only thought of him as Knox.

Her exquisite, kind, dreadful-at-chess lover.

He didn't stop by the Petal and Plume anymore, those random visits that had secretly brightened her day. With a fabricated cough, she concealed her smile behind the length of ribbon in her hand. An emerald green close to the color of a certain duke's eyes. He made no visits here because he appeared on her doorstep almost every *night*. Where they'd kiss until they were dizzy, then sneak up to her bedchamber. Or make their frantic way to the parlor. Once only going so far as the staircase, their clothing littered about her entryway. She'd sat atop his lap like she was mounting a horse. *Ride me*, he'd directed in that commanding tone he used when he was very, *very* aroused.

Clarissa sighed as heat rolled through her, settling between her thighs.

*La*, just the thought of Knox DeWitt did wicked things to her.

She nodded to let her customers know she'd noted their arrival. Although she didn't particularly like Countess Wimby and her companion, Miss Trenton. They were gossipy and condescending, typical of society matrons and their staff. However, Clarissa made bonnets for shrews as well as ladies. The hats sat the same, no matter the head.

Setting her ribbon aside, she picked up her quill and began making notations on a folio for her next order of fabric. Somewhere along the way, she found herself doodling *Clarissa DeWitt* in the margin. Three times before she stopped herself.

With a quick glance around her shop, she closed the folio with a snap.

If their affair had been what she'd envisioned, she would have been fine. Amorous negotiations only, and she might have been able to make it through the day without thinking about Knox a hundred times. However, they'd wrecked it with the meals and the jokes and the discussions about their childhoods. They frequently dined together at the small table wedged in the corner of her cozy kitchen, then climbed the stairs and snuggled beneath her woolen blankets, talking until they fell asleep. Sometimes they'd already made love, sometimes they waited until dawn. It was wonderful. Ordinary pleasures with an exceptional man. They had breakfast together, he reading *The Times*, she the *Gazette*. He liked fried eggs, and she was happy to accommodate.

Because her housekeeper, Mrs. Newton, only worked afternoon hours, they were able to share what Knox claimed to have never shared with anyone before.

Solitude.

Clarissa tapped her quill on the counter. He was witty, always making her laugh with stories about his brothers. And amiable even in the wee hours of the morning, a time when she was cranky without provocation. He seemed to find her brief bursts of irritability until she'd had her first cup of tea amusing. Despite having a turbulent past and a vile father, he was the kindest person she knew. He loved his family and acknowledged his obligations to his staff and his tenants without question.

She'd written three letters to him, absolving him of any responsibility toward *her*. Expressing in words that could not fully express how much their time had meant to her. Kissing the duke goodbye as she'd once flippantly called it.

Three notes she'd burned to a crisp in her hearth.

"Herschel will be at Lady Templeton's ball, I've been told," the countess whispered to her companion. "I should like a new bonnet in the event he shows, as he's been quite cagey of late, refusing most invitations. Something to set me apart from the female hordes in pursuit."

She snatched herself from her daydream to find Countess Wimby modeling a yellow capote bonnet in a beveled mirror. The color looked ghastly with her ginger hair and freckled skin, but Clarissa wasn't about to halt this conversation.

Miss Trenton, a distant cousin of some far-flung sort, preened and danced around the countess, giving the hat's brim a light tap. "Divine, simply divine. If anyone can capture a duke's attention, it would be you, my lady. Rumor has it His Grace is in the market for a wife."

The countess offered her companion a cheerless smile while Clarissa's blood churned. "He's in the market for a sizeable settlement, dear, his dwindling finances forcing his search for a duchess. The timing is perfect, nonetheless, as I've decided that the next time I marry, I'd like a man I fancy versus one old enough to be my grandfather. The Duke of Herschel is"—she sighed and fanned her face with her glove—"more attractive than one has a right to be while holding the oldest title in England. I can picture us being very happy together."

Clarissa pressed her hand to her stomach to suppress the queasy sensation rippling through it. The woman tying the ribbons of a gypsy bonnet beneath her chin across the room could be the next Duchess of Herschel. She would share Knox's bed. Touch him in the many wondrous ways Clarissa had. Watch his eyes cloud with bliss, his ardent release ringing through the night. She would watch him dip his toast in his tea while he hummed, a breakfast habit. She would argue with him about women's rights and the future of the House of Lords. She would have his children. His *children*.

Clarissa swallowed past the dizzying haze that spotted her vision.

These were more than feelings of possession, these were feelings of *love*.

She took a deep breath to calm herself, her mind spinning with the probability of misfortune. Unless she made her dreams come true—instead of waiting for a man to do it. Although her mother hadn't given her many words of advice, there was one statement that rang true.

*Fight for what you want, gel.*

∾

Knox had come to think of Clerkenwell as home.

Shaken by this sudden realization, he nodded mindlessly to the costermonger and waved to a group of children playing marbles on the corner. A

pression she'd worn the other times she'd met him. Which were precisely two. She didn't trust him, and he didn't blame her for it. He was renowned in ways he wished he wasn't. He also appreciated that she was trying to protect her employer in some small measure.

"Miss Marlowe isn't in at the moment," she said before he'd formulated one damned thing to say. Then, she made a move to shut the door practically in his face.

He wedged his Hoby boot neatly in the jamb to keep that from happening. "Did she leave a note for me, by any chance?"

"She did not, Your Grace."

His temper sparked. "I'll check the Petal and Plume, then."

She nodded without comment.

They stared across the narrow battlefield of an open doorway, his beaver hat taking the punishment for his unease. Reluctantly, he stepped away, drew a breath of London's frigid winter, and went back the way he'd come. West, to Mayfair.

His steps were trudging, and his heart was no longer light.

Crestfallen, he feared this rejection signaled the end of his grand love affair.

∼

Clarissa wandered Viscount Pemberly's indigo parlor, as his majordomo had called it when he'd settled her here. She'd had to travel to his Surrey country home for this discussion, a dwelling she'd never visited. The chamber was lovely, done in shades of sapphire that would make an impressive bonnet. Another servant had come to pour tea and serve gingerbread biscuits, flitting around like her visit was perfectly normal. The piquant scents mixed pleasantly with the cozy aroma of the hearthfire, a calming aspect she wished she could appreciate.

Perhaps she'd create an indigo-hued hat for the occasion of swallowing her pride whole. A celebratory accessory when one admitted hereditary defeat.

Sighing, Clarissa glanced at the mantel clock. Her father often used delay tactics to put her at a disadvantage. Thankfully, she was no longer young or impressionable enough to fall for such rubbish.

She hoped.

When the parlor door opened, and he marched through it seconds later, she suspected the world had changed in some way for him as well. He'd never come to her in less than a half hour.

Her stomach twisted to note their resemblance, a shock each time she saw him. Not enough of a similarity to alert society but enough for *her*. Enough for him, because he'd been unable to argue with her mother's claim about her parentage.

"Clarissa, what a pleasant surprise," he said in a dulcet tone and crossed to her. He dusted a kiss on each of her cheeks, a habit he'd acquired in France after his graduation from Eton. It always felt a bit forced to Clarissa, but suitable, as Viscount Pemberly wasn't known for his genuineness.

"Father," she returned, a moniker she used *only* in this home, per his instructions when she was five years old.

He gestured to the settee as he parked his large frame in the armchair across from her. She poured tea and served biscuits while he waited, both of them aware her ladylike graces had come from governesses paid for by him. It made her feel wonderful to know she'd finally found a use for the skills. Little did *he* understand this, however.

They nibbled and made idle conversation about the recent snowstorm, the tempest that had kept a duke trapped in her home for three delightful days. Of course, she'd been in love with Knox by the time he left. Likely, he'd planned it that way, the diabolical scoundrel.

The viscount pointed to her with his teacup. "You seem changed, dear girl. A soft smile and a more winsome demeanor. If only you'd found this maturity years ago, we might have gotten along better."

Clarissa shoved her wrath deep, in the chest she'd filled to the brim throughout her childhood. Although she must agree, she'd never been charming with this man. "You may disagree with your assessment after I tell you why I've come."

He froze, his cup and saucer shivering in his hand. Shaking his head with a breath shot through his nose, he slumped back in the armchair. "I can't say I'm surprised. Your mother didn't have a mind for commerce, either, though she tried, I will say. Skill with a needle and thread was about all she had going for her. I knew that little shop she left you would be in peril at some point."

Clarissa sipped tea and continued flashing her *soft* smile while she felt like a tigress inside. "The shop is actually doing well. Since I took over after Mother passed, I've tripled profits. What I've come to you about is a larger endeavor."

A lifelong pledge.

The viscount rocked forward, bracing his hands on his knees. "I'm sorry, dear girl, but I can't help you. I have two daughters on the Marriage Mart, and regrettably, they're not as attractive as you. Excellent lineages but grim countenances, the opposite of your situation. Their dowries are going to break me."

Clarissa glanced at him over the rim of her teacup, knowing this was not the case. "I've come to ask for a loan, not a grant. Two thousand pounds, with interest, payable in three years. My solicitor will draw up the contract and send it over if you agree. The shop will be yours if I fail to repay on time. The Petal and Plume is bringing in close to a thousand pounds a year. In fact, I've been thinking of hiring another milliner, growing my profit margin substantially. I have the clients for it. As it is, I turn trade away. I would go to a bank, but they'd laugh me out of the lobby, as you well know."

Pemberly snorted and slapped his knee. "That trivial twit of a ship is making a thousand a year? By God, I should get those silly offspring of mine sewing fripperies this minute! You clearly acquired your business acumen from me. Your mother lost money every blasted year."

Clarissa scooted to the edge of the settee, her hands trembling around her cup. "Will you agree?" She knew, despite his protestations, that he could well afford the risk, or she wouldn't have asked. "My offer is more than you'll make on any solid investment."

He grinned, showing a set of stained teeth, happiest when he had her over a barrel. "Desperate for cash, are you?"

He was going to do it. She knew by the bombastic expression on his face. Sitting back, relief washed over her, mitigating the burn to her pride. Knox DeWitt was worth every hint of pain. "I wouldn't say desperate. The funds are actually for my dowry." She decided to tell him because he would, along with the

## CHAPTER 7

WHERE A COUPLE FIND THEIR WAY

*C*larissa arrived at her cottage just after midnight to find a slumbering duke sprawled across her sofa. In fact, he was close to sliding off the piece and tumbling to the floor.

Laughing softly, she crossed to him with threads of love weaving through her heart. His jacket and greatcoat lay in a wad at his feet, his waistcoat and cravat scattered about. He'd unbuttoned his shirt, exposing the dark wisps of hair trailing to his belly. The bottle of whisky she'd bought last week sat, half-empty, on the table by his side. The chemist she'd purchased it from claimed that Islay, a Scottish island located in the Inner Hebrides, produced the best in the world.

She wanted her duke to have the finest of everything. Love did that to a girl.

Sighing, she went to her knee beside him. Hadn't he read the note she'd left with Mrs. Newton? The trip to Surrey and back was set to take the entire day, and she hadn't wanted him to worry. Nor had she wanted him to come along, even if he stayed in the carriage. Dealing with her father as a grown woman rather than an apprehensive child was an undertaking she had to accomplish on her own.

The visit had gone better than she'd anticipated. She'd cut the strings to one life and tied them to another. Walked away from a past that didn't deserve more contemplation.

"Knox, darling," she whispered into his ear. She pressed a kiss to his lips and took a joyous breath. He smelled of her expensive Scotch, leather, and the faint scent of vetiver.

He murmured sleepily, reaching around her to draw her close. "I'm dreaming."

Tickling her nose against his cheek, she smiled. "No, you're not."

He blinked, slumber flowing from his eyes. They were wide and *oh*, so green. Like blades of grass in the spring. She'd never tire of gazing into them. "I thought you'd left me."

She thrust aside the flicker of irritation with her housekeeper. He'd never gotten her note. Mrs. Newton was only protecting her from a powerful man she assumed was going to bring her employer trouble. Like the rest of the world, the two souls in this room were the only ones who'd ever understand. Cradling his jaw, she turned his lips to hers. The caress was soft, tender, and knowing. "Why would I ever leave you?"

Turning in a fury to his side, he caught her face in his hands and swept her into the most possessive kiss of their relationship. She fell into him, over him, where they tussled, fighting to deepen an embrace that merely ended with them toppling to the floor.

"Heavens, you're heavy," she whispered in a gusting gasp.

He shifted to bring her under his long body, nudging a table away irritably with his boot. "You've always liked it before," he said against her lips, trying to dive in where they'd left off before the tumble.

Alas, she knew where *this* would end up. They were the worst two for maintaining decorum once the kissing started.

She pushed his chest, forcing him back. "Knox, I have to talk to you."

He paused, that haunted look returning to his face. Her heart ached for the boy who'd been so easily disregarded that the man thought it was an available option. "I don't know if I want to hear this. If I can."

Wiggling from beneath him, she hushed him by placing her hand over his mouth, where he promptly gave her a good nip with his teeth. "Ouch, you arrogant beast!"

He rose to his feet, exhaled sharply, and began to pace the room. He made it to the chess set where he fiddled with a pawn, a queen, then a rook. His instruction was ongoing, though his play had not improved.

Settling against the settee, Clarissa let him fidget. For a minute or more before she spoke. "I have a proposal to make."

Halting, he propped his hip against the escritoire they'd nearly taken down that first night. She would never be able to work there without thinking about him exploring the most intimate parts of her and making them blossom, coming to *life*. His lessons had been thorough and welcome. For this, too, she thanked him.

He'd captured not only her mind and heart—but her body.

He whipped his hand in a fast circle and gave his bootheel a pop on the carpeted floor. "Out with it. You're killing me in slow degrees. A thousand cuts, don't they say?"

Drawing her legs to her chest, she arranged her skirt carefully around her. She didn't need him going off-course. There was plenty of time for that *after* they'd decided their future.

Although Knox's gaze tracked her like he held a bow in his hands and she was the target. He swallowed, shifting his legs to hide a reaction there was no use trying to hide, the darling man. "I'm losing focus, love, I have to admit. Maybe it's the whisky. Or maybe it's simply you."

She smiled, pleased. Lifting her skirt, she gave him a brief, tantalizing view.

He groaned, but took her signal, staying where he was. His shaft, however, was an impressive sight, tenting his trousers.

*Out with it, Clarissa*, she reminded herself.

Hugging her knees, she propped her chin atop them. Nerves were racing through her belly and zipping out her trembling hands. "I went to visit my father. That's where I was all day. He's in the country, in Surrey."

Knox cursed, impatience he rarely showed roaring to life. Growling, he shoved off the desk. "You went to bloody Surrey without me? To see that blackguard?"

"This was my battle to fight, Knox, not yours."

His chest fell on a sigh. "Why, Clari? *Why* did you go to him?"

*Clari*. She treasured the endearment. He'd said it the first time while they were making love eight short days ago, a moment burned into her memory. "Because I love you more than I'd imagined I could love someone. Because I'm happy, truly happy. Because I want to have your children, I want to be your *wife*, not your mistress. A situation that would destroy us. And I was getting desperate enough to consider it."

Clarissa pressed a smile into her knotted fingers at his thunderstruck expression.

*By heaven*, she'd done the impossible.

She'd silenced Knoxville DeWitt.

His gaze dropped as his lips moved, although the crackle of the hearthfire was the only sound in the room. When he looked back, she was entranced to see his cheeks were flushed, his eyes bright with what she suspected were tears.

"I—" He coughed into his fist, and rocked from boot to boot before he strode across the room. Dropping to his haunches before her, he rolled his bottom lip between his teeth and tried again. "I came here today to ask you the same question. Last night, in the moonlight, you sleeping, with my body and mind sated, I decided I could not, *would* not, live without you. I'm not willing to let my obligations rule this aspect of my life when it rules so many others. I love you endlessly, beyond measure. There is, in fact, *no* measure. Then, despite my impulsive planning, blast all independent chits, you end up asking first."

She grasped his hand, winding her fingers through his. He hung on, tightly enough to let her know he was never letting go. "I *had* to ask, Knox. Because I won't have you believing you've made a sacrifice for me."

His gaze narrowed, his grip tensing. "You're worth any sacrifice, Clari. Don't you understand that?"

"It was only my pride, darling, which in the end is hardly worth mentioning."

He let her go, bracing his hands on his knees, but he didn't leave her. "You asked Pemberly for your dowry."

# EPILOGUE

Although there were occasional brotherly fisticuffs and gentlemanly brawls, the Troublesome Trio had died a contented death, with all parties involved the happier for it.

Because they were now a family of ten.

Cort and Alex had two girls, Kathleen and Caroline. Damien and Mercy had contributed to the total with the arrival of Crispin and Quincy last fall. (After all, twins ran in the family.)

In three months, he and Clari would make it a breathtaking, incredible *eleven*.

Knox placed his whisky on the balustrade as happiness rippled over him like a gentle breeze. As they were wont to do these days, the DeWitt clan was gathered at the family estate in Hampstead. They spent every summer here, away from the strife and smog in London. Away from the responsibilities and the demands. The Duke of Herschel dropped his mantle in the country, becoming what he'd always wanted to be, a man. Clarissa DeWitt's befuddled but forever besotted husband. Brother. Uncle.

It was no lie to say that his entire world was out there on the lawn.

Damien's wife, Mercy, was sitting on a woolen blanket, her pad balanced on her knees. She was sketching the scene laid out before her, an admittedly lovely one. Her husband was stretched out beside her, a book in his hand, a sleeping baby curled under his arm. Cort and his wife, Alex, were racing the children around the archery target, directing their every move, thankfully the only battlefield his brother would ever see again.

And then there was the light of his life.

As if she'd heard his thoughts, Clarissa glanced at him, her smile radiant. Her hand was curved over her rounded belly, her habit of late. She blew him a kiss, then turned, laughing, when the children sprinted toward her. Sunlight danced along the ivory strands cascading over her shoulders. Here, she let her hair down in more ways than one.

Sometimes, reminiscences of his father intruded, but they grew fainter with every wonderful memory he filled his life with. His past was disappearing into the mist of his future.

Therefore, when the children dashed over, begging a duke to join them in play, Knox jumped right in.

*The End*

# THANK YOU!

Thank you for coming along on Knox and Clarissa's romantic ride! I really *love* writing about brothers, as anyone who reads my books knows! (The Garretts, anyone?) If you'd like to check out the rest of the Troublesome Trio, Damien's love story appears in *The Devil of Drury Lane* and Cort's in *Kiss the Rake Hello*.

*Kiss the Rake Hello* features an age-gap reversal with the heroine the older one this time! And *The Devil of Drury Lane* was my first virgin hero!

Next in line in the popular Duchess Society series is Jasper Noble's wicked tale, *Three Sins and a Scoundrel*. I can promise second chance, second chance, second chance! My favorite trope. If you're reading the series, you know that Jasper has a lot of secrets—and a lovely heart beneath the bluster.

Please sign up for my newsletter at www.tracysumner.com. You'll receive a free read (the award-winning novella, *Chasing the Duke*) as my thank you. The cover is hot, hot, hot, as is the story! I also have a Facebook reader's group, The Contrary Countesses. Join me for the steamy fun!

## THANK YOU!

Happy reading, as always! Historical romance is the best.

xoxo

# CHAPTER ONE

*Limehouse Basin, London, 1822*

She'd taken this assignment on a dare.

A dare to herself.

Unbridled curiosity had driven her, the kind that killed cats. When it was just another promise-of-rain winter day. Another dismal society marriage the Duchess Society was overseeing.

Another uninspiring man to investigate.

Hildegard Templeton told herself everything was normal. The warehouse had looked perfectly ordinary from the grimy cobblestones her post-chaise deposited her on. A sign swinging fearlessly in the briny gust ripping off the Thames—*Streeter, Macauley & Company*—confirming she'd arrived at the correct location. A standard, salt-wrecked dwelling set amongst tea shops and taverns, silk merchants and ropemakers. Surrounded by shouting children, overladen carts, horses, dogs, vendors selling sweetmeats and pies, and the slap of sails against ships' masts. A chaotic but essential locality, with cargo headed all over England but landing in this grubby spit of dockyard first.

# CHAPTER ONE

When she'd stepped inside, she halted in place, realizing her blunder in assuming anything about Tobias Streeter was *normal*.

Hildy knew nothing about architecture but knew this was not the norm for a refurbished warehouse bordering the Limehouse Basin Lock. A suspect neighborhood her post-boy hadn't been pleased to drive into—or be asked to wait *in* while she conducted her business. Honestly, the building was a marvel of iron joists, girders, and cast-iron columns with ornamental heads. With a splash of elegant color—crimson and black. What she imagined a gentleman's club might look like, a refined yet dodgy sensibility she found utterly... *charming*. And entirely unnecessary for a building housing a naval merchant's headquarters.

Her exhalation left her in a vaporous cloud, and she gazed around with a feeling she didn't like as the piquant scent of a spice she identified as Asian in origin enveloped her.

A feeling she wasn't accustomed to.

Miscalculation.

As she would admit only to her business partner, Georgiana, the newly minted Duchess of Markham: *I fear I've botched the entire project*. She'd taken society's slander as truth—shipping magnate, Romani blood, profligate bounder, and the most noteworthy moniker the *ton* had ever come up with—and made up her mind about the man, concocting a wobbly plan unsupported by proper research. A proposal built on assumptions instead of *fact*. Sloppy dealings were very unlike her. Ambition to secure the agreement to advise the Earl of Hastings's five daughters as they traveled along their matrimonial journey— the eldest currently set on marrying the profligate bounder—had risen above common sense.

## CHAPTER ONE

brandy or scotch, another misstep had she presumed it.

When, of course, she'd presumed it.

As he patiently accepted her appraisal, his hand rose, and his index finger, just the calloused tip, trailed her cheek to tuck a stray strand behind her ear.

The hands of a man who worked with them.

*Played* with them.

She shivered, a shallow exhalation she couldn't contain rushing forth in a steamy puff. Parts of the ground story were open from quay to yard for transit handling, and glacial gusts were whistling through like a train on tracks.

"Alton," he instructed without glancing away from her, though he dropped his hand to his side. "Close the doors at the back, will you? And bring tea to my office."

"Tea," Alton echoed. "*Tea?*"

Streeter's breath fanned her face, warming her to her toes. "Isn't that what ladies drink over business dealings? If ladies even *do* business. Perhaps it's what they drink over spirited discussions about watercolors or their latest gown."

She gripped the folio until her knuckles ached, feeling like a ball of yarn being tossed between two cats. "Make no special accommodations. I'll have whatever it is you guzzle during business dealings, Mr. Streeter."

He laughed, then caught himself with the slightest downward tilt of his lips. She'd surprised them both somehow. It was the first chess move she'd won in this match. "We guzzle malt whiskey then," he murmured and turned, seeming to expect her to follow.

She recorded details as she shadowed him across

## CHAPTER ONE

the vast space crowded with shipping crates and assorted stacks of rope and tools, to a small room at the back overlooking the pier. His shirt was untucked on one side, the kerchief he'd wiped his face with slapping his thigh. His clothing was finely made but not skillfully enough to hide a muscular build most men used built-in padding to establish. Dark hair, *no*, more than dark. Black as tar, curling over his rumpled shirt collar and around his ears. So pitch dark, she imagined she could see cobalt streaks in it, like a flame gone mad.

Hair that called a woman's fingers to tangle in it, no matter the woman.

The gods had allotted this conceited beast an inequitable share of beauty, that was certain. And for the first time in her *life*, Hildy was caught up in an attraction.

His office was another unsurprising surprise.

A roaring fire in the hearth chasing away the chill. A Carlton House desk flanked by two armchairs roomy enough to fit Streeter or his man of business, Alton. A Hepplewhite desk, or a passable imitation. A colorful Aubusson covering the floor, nothing threadbare and old because it had lost its value. Her heart skipped as she stepped inside the space, confirmation that she'd indeed misjudged. Shelf upon shelf of leather-bound books bracketed the walls. Walking to a row, she checked the spines with a searching review. Cracked but good, each and every one of them. Architecture, commerce, mathematics, chemistry. Nothing entertaining, nothing playful. The library of a man with a mind.

While Streeter moved to a sideboard that had likely come from the king's castoffs, and poured them a drink from a bottle whose label she didn't recognize, she circled the room, inspecting.

Holding both glasses in one hand, he situated

# CHAPTER ONE

himself not at his desk but on the edge of an overturned crate beside it, his long legs stretched before him. Sipping from his while holding hers, his steely gaze tracked her. Fortunately, she realized from the travel-weary Wellington he tapped lightly on the carpet, her examination of his private space was making him uneasy. With an aggrieved grunt, he yanked the kerchief from his waistband and tossed it needlessly to the floor.

Finally, she sighed in relief, a *weakness*. If he didn't like to be studied, he must have *something* to hide. She'd been hired, in part, to find out what.

"This isn't one of your frivolous races through the park." He leaned to place her glass on the corner of his desk. Hers to take, or not, when she passed. The only charitable thing he'd done was pour it for her. "Right now, I have two men guarding your traveling chariot parked outside, lest someone rob you blind. The thing is as yellow as a ripe banana, which catches the eye. They'll slice the velvet from the squabs and resell it two blocks over for fast profit. Your post-boy looked ready to expire when we got to him. Guessing he's never had to sit on his duff while waiting for his mistress to complete business in the East End. A slightly larger *man* might better fit the bill next time."

*Post-boys were all she could afford.*

Hildy released the satin chin strap and slid her bonnet from her head. Her coiffure, unsteady on a good day as her maid's vision was dreadful, collapsed with the removal, and a wave of hair just a shade darker than the sun fell past her shoulders. Streeter blinked, his fingers tightening around his glass. She noticed the insignificant gesture while wondering if the fevered awareness filling the air was only in *her* mind.

Halting by his desk, she reached for her drink

## CHAPTER ONE

with a nod in his direction. The scent of soap and spice drifted to her, his unique mix. "This warehouse, it's quite unusual. Magnificent, actually. I've never seen the like."

"I'll be sure to tell the architect the daughter of an earl approves." His gaze cool, giving away absolutely nothing, he dug a bamboo toothpick from his trouser pocket and jammed it between his teeth, working it from side to side between a pair of very firm lips. At her raised brow, he shrugged. "Stopped smoking. It's enough to breathe London's coal-laden air without asking for more trouble."

Hildy dropped the folio, which held little of value aside from her employment contract with the Earl of Hastings, in the armchair and lifted the glass to her lips. The whiskey was smooth, smoky—*good*. "This is excellent," she mused, licking her lips and watching Streeter's hand again tense around his tumbler.

"Thank you. It's my own formula," he said after a charged silence, a dent appearing next to his mouth. Not so much a dimple. Two of which she had herself, a feature people had commented on her entire life.

His was more of an elevated smirk.

"Yours?" Continuing her journey around the room, Hildy paused by a framed blueprint of this warehouse. Beside it was another detailed sketch, a building she didn't recognize. Architectural schematics drawn by someone very talented. She couldn't miss the initials, *TS*, in the lower right corner.

Frowning, she tilted her glass, staring into it as if the amber liquor would provide answers to an increasingly enigmatic puzzle. Aside from disappointing her family and society, she'd never done anything remarkable. *Been* anything remarkable.

## CHAPTER ONE

When faced with remarkability, she wasn't sure she trusted it.

Streeter stacked his boots one atop the other, the crate creaking beneath him. "A business venture, a distillery going south financially that I found myself uncommonly intrigued by, once I handed over an astounding amount of blunt to keep it afloat *and* demanded I be invited into the process. Usually, I invest, then step away if the enterprise is well-managed, which it often isn't, but this…" Bringing the glass to his lips, he drank around the toothpick. Quite a feat. She couldn't look away from the show of masculine bravado if she'd been ordered to at the end of a pistol. "It's straightforward chemistry, the brewing of malt. But, lud, what a challenge, seeking perfection."

Finessing his glass into an empty spot next to him on the crate, he wiggled the toothpick from his lips and pointed it at her. A crude signal that he was ready to begin negotiations. "Isn't seeking perfection your business too, luv? The *ideal* bloke, without shortcomings. I've yet to see such a man, but the Mad Matchmaker is fabled to work miracles, so maybe there's a chance for me."

Seating herself in the chair absent her paperwork, Hildy set her glass on the desk and worked her gloves free, one deliberate finger at a time. If he believed he could chase her away with his bullying attitude, he hadn't done suitable research into his opponent's background. Last year, the Duchess Society had completed an assignment, confidential in nature but rumored nonetheless, for the royal family. Madness, power, fantastic wealth, love gained, love lost. This handsome scoundrel and his trifling reach for society's acceptance, she could handle.

# CHAPTER ONE

Although she realized she was silently reminding herself of the fact, not stating it outright.

"Nothing to do with perfection and rarely anything to do with love, Mr. Streeter. The betrothals I support are, like the marriage you're proposing with Lady Matilda Delacour-Baynham, a business agreement. Unless I'm mistaken from the discussions I've had with her and her father, the Earl of Hastings."

He twirled the toothpick between his fingers like a magician. "You have it dead on. Holy hell, I'm not looking for love. Don't fill the chit's head with that rubbish. The words mean nothing to me. They never have. Society only sells the idea to make the necessity of unions such as these more acceptable."

Well, *that* sounded personal. "Lady Matilda—"

"Mattie wants freedom. If you know her, she's told you what she's interested in. The only thing. Medicine." He laughed and sent the toothpick spinning. "An earl's daughter, can you conjure it? When no female can be a physician and certainly not a legitimate lady. To use one of your brethren's expressions, it's beyond the pale."

He winked at her, *winked*, and she was reasonably certain he didn't mean it playfully.

"I have funds, more than she can spend in a lifetime. More than I can. She wants to use a trifling bit to rescue her father, a man currently drowning, and I do mean drowning, in debt? Fine. Finance her hobby of practicing medicine? Also fine. Or her *dream*, if you're the visionary sort. Let her safely prowl these corridors and others on the rookery trail, delivering babes, bandaging wounds, swabbing fevered brows. They have no one else, the desperate souls I live amongst. She'll be an angel in their midst. And me, the one controlling the deliverance. Deliverance for *her* from your upmarket bunch. Who, other than

## CHAPTER ONE

finding ways to creatively lose capital, do nothing but sit around on their arses making up nicknames for those who *prosper*."

"What's in it for you?" Hildy whispered, not sure she knew. Was Tobias Streeter, rookery bandit, shipping titan, this eager to marry into a crowd that indeed sat on their toffs all day dreaming up pointless monikers? When she'd been trying to escape them her entire *life*?

He jabbed the toothpick in her direction, his smile positively savage. "Don't worry about what I need. I don't make deals where I don't profit, luv."

A caged tiger set loose on society. That's what he was. Half of London was secretly fawning over him while refusing him admittance to their sacred drawing rooms.

Not so fussy about admittance to their beds, she'd bet.

He slipped the toothpick home between his stubbornly compressed lips. "Templeton, you of all people should understand her predicament, being somewhat peculiar yourself. Boxed in by society's expectations, unless I'm missing my guess, which I usually don't. I understand, do you see? It's why the girl trusts me. Why, maybe, I trust *her*.

"I know what it's like to be found lacking for elements beyond your control. Where you were born, the color of your skin. Being delivered on the wrong side of some addled viscount's blanket. Think nothing of intelligence or courage, wit or ingenuity, *talent*, only the blue blood, or lack of it, running beneath that no one sees unless you slice them open."

Hildy smoothed her hand down her bodice and laid her gloves in a neat tangle on her knee, Streeter chasing every move with his intense, sea-green gaze. That blasted blue blood he spoke of kept her tangled

## CHAPTER ONE

in a web, day in and day out. He didn't need to enlighten her. Resignedly, she nodded to the folio lying like a spent weapon between them.

"Let's discuss specifics, shall we? Hastings wants you to court his daughter properly. Even if Lady... um, Mattie doesn't require it, *he* does. Flowers, gifts, trinkets. Courtship rituals. The servants gossip, and everyone in London then knows what's what, so this is an essential, seemingly trivial part of the process. I'll assist with the selection. He'd also like certain businesses you're involved with downplayed, so to speak. The unsavory enterprises. At least until the first babe is born. Rogue King of Limehouse Basin isn't exactly what he desired for his darling girl. But you, obviously, got to her first."

"At least I'm not an ivory-turner," he whispered beneath his breath.

She tilted her head in confusion.

"Her father cheats at dice, my naïve hoyden. I do many cursed things, but cheating is not one. Every gaming hell in town is after him." Streeter growled and, snatching up his glass, polished off the contents. Lord, she wished he'd button his collar. The view was becoming a distraction. "There's more to this agreement. I can see from the brutal twist of those comely lips of yours. More edges to be smoothed away like sandpaper to rough timber. Go on, spit it out. I can take a ruthless assessment."

Hildy controlled, through diligence born of her own beatdowns, the urge to raise her hand to cover her lips. *Comely* ones that had begun to sting pleasantly at his backhanded compliment. "Aside from your agreement that my solicitors—in addition to yours and the earl's—will review all contracts to ensure fairness for both parties, there is the matter of Miss Henson."

## CHAPTER ONE

He whispered a curse against crystal and was unapologetic when his narrowed gaze met hers. He lowered his glass until it rested on his flat belly. "So, I'm to play the holy man until the ceremony?" Then he muttered something she didn't catch. Or didn't want to. *For a wife who prefers women.*

Hildy made a mental note to investigate that disastrous possibility, although it made no difference. Lady Matilda—Mattie—had to get married to someone. A *male* someone. Why not this beautiful devil who seemed to actually *like* her? Heavens, Hildy thought in despair. The Duchess Society couldn't weather the storm should a scandal of that magnitude come to light. It was illegal, which was absurd, of course, but that was the case. There were whisperings of such goings-on, relationships on the sly.

Rumors with the power to destroy one's *life*.

It was decided at that moment, with dust motes swirling through fading wintry sunlight, in a startlingly elegant office in the middle of a slum. This marriage, between a lady who wanted to be a doctor but couldn't and a tenacious blackguard who wanted high society tucked neatly in his pocket, had to happen. Or Hildy and her enterprise to save the women of London from gross matrimonial injustice was *finished*.

Too, she would go belly up without funds coming in to pay the bills—and coming in *soon*.

Streeter rocked forward, his Wellingtons dusting the floor, upsetting the shipping crate until she feared it would collapse beneath him. "I return the question because it's a valuable one. Besides a hefty fee that Hastings can't afford and will eventually derive from other sources, namely the source sharing this stale malt air with you, what's in it for you? Dealing with me isn't going to be easy. Ask my part-

## CHAPTER ONE

ners, should you be able to locate them. Mattie isn't much better from what I know of her. Her spirit is part of the reason I believed she'd be the right woman for the job."

Hildy chewed on her bottom lip, an abominable habit, then glanced up to find Streeter's gaze had gone vacant around the edges. The way a man's does when he's *thinking* about things. She wasn't, saints above, imagining the thread of attraction strung between them like ship's netting. He felt it, too. "I'll be candid."

"Please do," he whispered, bringing himself back from his musing, his cheeks slightly tinged. His breathing maybe, *maybe*, churning faster.

"When I arrived, I would've said I was doing it to secure future business with the Earl of Hastings. He has five daughters, as you know, and no wife to guide them. A line of inept governesses, another quitting every week it seems. My proposal?

"I guide him to appropriate men for the remaining four since Mattie has you on the hook. *Decent* men my people have investigated thoroughly. Then assist with the negotiations, so his daughters are protected, pay my coal bill, and we're both happy." Hildy ran her finger over a nap in the chair's velvet, her gaze dropping to record her progress. "Frankly, I need the money as I wasn't left a large inheritance, more a burden. An ever-maturing residence and staff and no funds allocated for preservation.

"And I'm not planning to marry myself, so survival falls directly to me. Likewise, I do this to benefit the young women I work with, if you must know, not simply as a business venture. You have no idea how lacking they are simply from being isolated from any discussions outside the appropriate tea to serve.

# CHAPTER ONE

They're forced to sign contracts they can't even begin to understand—*lifelong*, binding contracts—with no assistance."

The toothpick bounced in Streeter's mouth as he bit down on it. "What's changed?"

Digging her fingertips into the chair's cushion, she decided to tell him. "I'm *bored* with earls and viscounts in fretful need of an heir to carry on a line that should cease production. In need of capital to salvage a crumbling empire. A rumored Romani bastard who's hiding what he really wants, and I'm the person hired to find out what?" She snapped her fingers, a weight lifting as she spoke the truth. "Now, there's a challenge."

For a breathless second, Streeter's face erased of expression. Like a fist swept across a mirror's vapor. She'd stunned him—and her pulse soared. Foolishly, categorically. Then a broad smile, a *sincere* smile, sent the dent in his cheek pinging. His teeth flashed in wonderfully startling contrast to his olive skin. "Well, damn, I can be surprised." He saluted her with the glass he'd picked up only to find it empty. "A worthy opponent steps out of the mist."

"I'm not an opponent," she murmured, knowing she was.

With a sigh of regret, perhaps because she'd gone back to fibbing, he braced his hand on his thigh and rose to his feet. She watched him cross the room because she couldn't help herself. Tall, broad yet lean, an awe-inspiring physique even in mussed clothing. He moved with an innate grace even a duke wouldn't necessarily have possessed. Natural and unassuming. The stuff one was born with—or without. Elegance that simply was.

He stopped before another of the schematic drawings, an imposing brick structure laid out with

## CHAPTER ONE

mathematical precision she suspected existed only in the sketch. "What if I say no to working with you? Refuse your kind service. Toss it back to Hastings like a flaming ember, pitting his desperation against my ambition."

Hildy understood after a moment's panic that this was part of the negotiation. That the correct response, or non-response, was vital. Retrieving her glass, she took a generous pull, smooth liquor chasing away the chill. "Is it any different than working with your"—she gestured over her shoulder to the warehouse—"bountiful trading partners? We'll be in business together. End of story."

He paused, studying her in a way few men had dared to even while telling her how beautiful she was. Men she'd never wanted to undress her with their eyes, as the saying went. A phrase that until this second had held no meaning.

A peculiar tension, the awareness from earlier, roared between them as if Alton had reopened the doors and let the Thames rush in. As if Tobias Streeter had laid his hands on her. An experience she had no familiarity with which to visualize.

"End of story," he murmured joylessly and turned back to his sketch.

She deposited her folio on his desk, the thump ringing through the room. Outside, a dockworker's shout and the rub and bump of a ship sliding into harbor pierced the hush. He was equally damaged, she could see. And very good at hiding it. They were alike in this regard, a mysterious element only another wounded animal would recognize.

Making the call on instinct alone, Hildy nonetheless made it.

Tobias Streeter wasn't a fiend. He wasn't an abuser like her father.

## CHAPTER ONE

He was just a man.

A man she was willing to polish until he shone like the crown jewels. "There will be events. Part of your engagement and introduction to the *ton*, as it were. You'll likely need some instruction."

He tapped the sketch three times before shifting to lean his shoulder against the wall in a negligent slump she no longer counted as factual. "I clean up well. Never fear," he said, his voice laced with scorn. Who it was directed at, she wasn't sure. "I'll review the contract in that tasteful folio of yours this evening, then we'll discuss the details tomorrow afternoon. I'll send a carriage with a coachman ready to protect you should the need arise, not those lads just out of the schoolroom you have manning your conveyance."

Glancing to a clock on the mantel that had been cautiously ticking off time, his smile thinned, frigid enough to freeze water. "I'm sorry to rush you out, but I have a meeting in ten minutes that will, if successful, net me close to a thousand pounds. My men will escort you home. Your chariot can follow along for fun." His jaw tensed when she started to argue, and he pushed off the wall with a growl. "Not on my watch, Templeton. Not in my township. Don't even *begin*."

However, stubborn chit that she was, she did begin, opening her mouth to tell him who was managing this campaign to show London how bloody wonderful a husband he would be.

"Tea and some of them lemony biscuits from the baker on the corner, coming right up," Alton proclaimed, stumbling into the room, a silver teapot she wondered where in heaven's name he'd located clutched in a meaty fist and two mismatched china cups balanced in the other. Halting, he took one look at his employer's thunderous expression, slapped the cups on the first available surface, and hustled Hildy from the office.

The teapot was still in his hand as Streeter's coach rolled down the congested lane with her an unwilling captive inside. She suppressed a clumsy laugh to see a coat of arms, painted over but visible, on the carriage's door.

Another aristocrat who'd lost his fortune to the Rogue King.

Hildy collapsed against the plush squabs of the finest transport she'd ever ridden in, realizing she hadn't asked Tobias Streeter how he planned to profit from a marriage he didn't want.

# ABOUT TRACY

*USA Today* bestselling author Tracy's story telling career began when she picked up a copy of LaVyrle Spencer's Vows on a college beach trip. A journalism degree and a thousand romance novels later, she decided to try her hand at writing a southern version of the perfect love story. With a great deal of luck and more than a bit of perseverance, she sold her first novel to Kensington Publishing.

When not writing sensual stories featuring complex characters and lush settings, Tracy can be found reading romance, snowboarding, watching college football and figuring out how she can get to 100 countries before she kicks. She lives in the south, but after spending a few years in NYC, considers herself a New Yorker at heart.

Tracy has been awarded the National Reader's Choice, the Write Touch and the Beacon—with finalist nominations in the HOLT Medallion, Heart of Romance, Rising Stars and Reader's Choice. Her books have been translated into German, Dutch, Portuguese and Spanish. She loves hearing from readers about why she tends to pit her hero and heroine against each other from the very first page or that great romance she simply must order.

Connect with Tracy on http://www.tracy-sumner.com